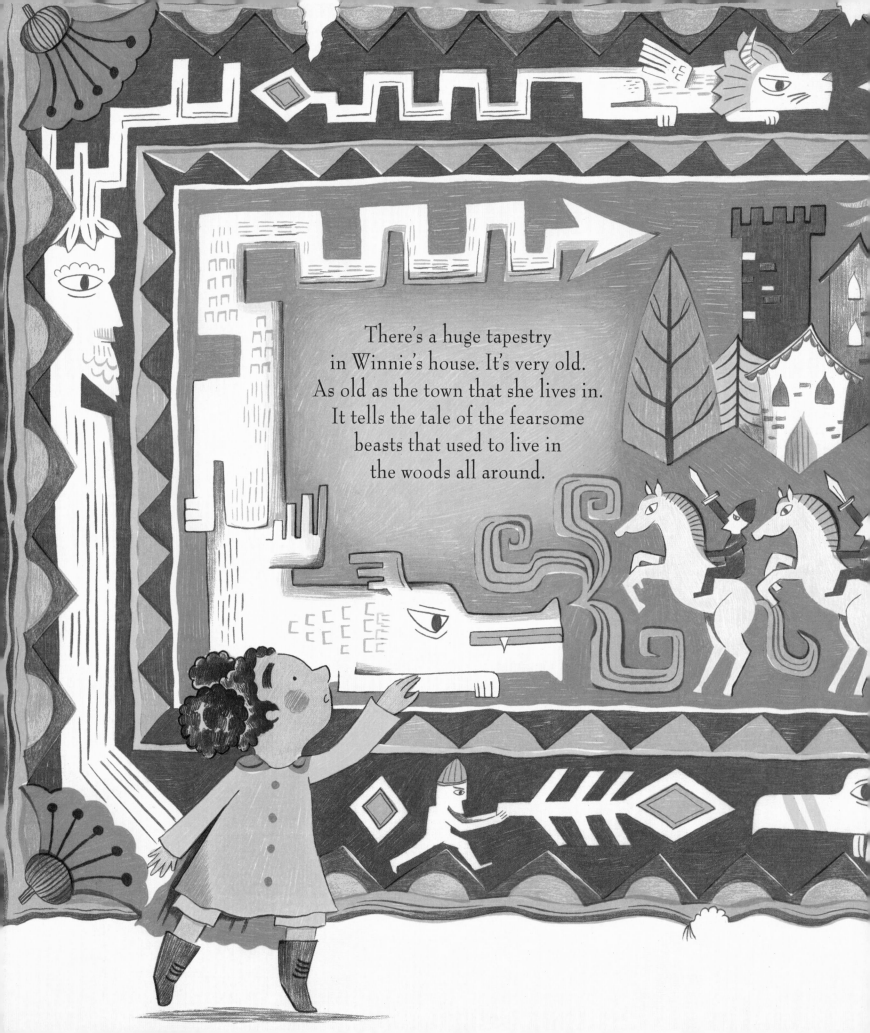

There's a huge tapestry
in Winnie's house. It's very old.
As old as the town that she lives in.
It tells the tale of the fearsome
beasts that used to live in
the woods all around.

Winnie touched the sharp teeth of the dragon. "Do you think they'll ever come back?" she asked.

"No," said her parents. "Our grandparents fought a great battle, and now they're gone."

That night, like most nights, Winnie dreamed of dragons.

And that night, like most nights, she woke to a BOOM and a RUMBLE and a FLASH!

"The dragons are back!"
she cried. "I can hear them snoring!"
But her parents called, "It's just a storm.
Go back to sleep."

So Winnie slept – but her dreams
were still full of dragons.

All next day, she practised with her wooden sword.
"Just in case a dragon comes," she said.

Suddenly the wind started to howl.

"Winnie! Come in now!"
called her mum. "There's a storm coming!"

Winnie looked up at the sky.
It didn't look stormy.
But then . . .

. . . a huge gust of wind
swept her up into the air, tumbling
and twisting over the treetops.

"Help me!" she cried.
She was soaring over the hills
when she started to fall.

Down and
down she went, until
WHOOSH!
she landed on the
back of . . .

. . . an
actual
dragon!

The dragon set her
down gently in a faraway clearing.
"You DO still exist!" she gasped. "I knew it!"
"I do," said the dragon. "Sorry if I swept
you off your feet. Sometimes
I flap my wings too hard."

The next moment, they heard a loud rumbling
and shuffling through the trees.
"Aha!" said the dragon. "You
can meet my friends, too."

Winnie looked up at three extraordinary faces.
"I've seen you on the tapestry!" she cried.

But the creatures
just frowned at her.
"Why did you bring her
here?" growled the lion.
"You know humans always
hurt us," said the gryphon.
"Look! She has a sword!"
said the tree man.

Winnie threw down her sword. "I'd never hurt you!"
"Don't mind them," said the dragon.
"It's just we're the last of our kind,
so we have to stay secret."

"I only want to be friends,"
said Winnie.

So, for the rest of that
day, she did what friends do.

She decorated the tree man
with flowers.

She collected the tastiest apples for the gryphon.

And, as the sun set, she gave the winged lion's back a good long scratch.

"Where do you sleep?" she asked. "We don't," said the lion. "At night-time humans are asleep, and that's when we can . . .

". . . go wild! Have a beastly bash! And a hullabaloo!" As the creatures danced, Winnie gasped in amazement. It was the noises she heard every night!

FLASH!

BOOM!

RUMBLE!

Winnie
danced with her
fantastical friends
till the forest shook.
Then, suddenly . . .

. . . the sound of horse's hooves echoed through the hills,
and a voice shouted, "Winnie! Where are you?"

"That's my dad! I have to go home now."
"But you can't go home!" said the gryphon.
"You have to stay with us now, or the humans will find us."

Winnie was horrified.

"We're the last ones left,"
said Tree Man, "so we have
to be kept secret."

"Can you keep a secret?" asked
the dragon, doubtfully.

Winnie stood tall.
"Of course I can! You're my friends,
and I'd never let you down."

"In that case," said the gryphon, "we'll take you home.
But we shall have to be quiet as mice."

Tree Man kept lookout and they snuck through the valleys,

until they saw the town through the trees.

Then it was
time to say goodbye.
"I'll keep your secret for ever,"
said Winnie.

Winnie's parents searched for hours.
Suddenly, in the distance, they saw a light come
on in their home. "Perhaps she's back?" they cried.

And she was!

"Where have you been? We've been so worried." But Winnie was too tired to say. "I think it's bedtime," said her mum.

That night, like most nights, they all woke to a BOOM and a RUMBLE and a FLASH!

BOOM!! FLASH!! RUMBLE!

"Perhaps the dragons are back!" cried her parents. "We can hear them snoring!"

"It's just a storm," said Winnie. "Go back to sleep."

So they slept
– and their dreams were
full of dragons.

For Helen, Alison and Zoë
Thank you for filling me with self-belief and taking me
into new and totally fantastical directions!

First published in the UK in 2021 by Alison Green Books
An imprint of Scholastic Children's Books
Euston House, 24 Eversholt Street London NW1 1DB
A division of Scholastic Ltd
www.scholastic.co.uk
London – New York – Toronto – Sydney – Auckland – Mexico City – New Delhi – Hong Kong
Designed by Zoë Tucker
Text and illustrations copyright © 2021 Melissa Castrillón
HB ISBN: 978 1 407194 48 6 • PB ISBN: 978 1 407194 49 3
Printed in Malaysia
1 3 5 7 9 10 8 6 4 2
The moral rights of Melissa Castrillón have been asserted.
Papers used by Scholastic Children's Books are made from wood grown in sustainable forests